LIANG and the MAGIC PAINTBRUSH

by DEMI

Henry Holt and Company / New York

To Jesse

Henry Holt and Company, LLC
Publishers since 1866
175 Fifth Avenue
New York, New York 10010
www.henryholtchildrensbooks.com

Henry Holt® is a registered
trademark of Henry Holt and Company, LLC.

Library of Congress Cataloging-in-Publication Data
Demi / Liang and the magic paintbrush
Summary: A poor boy who longs to paint is given
a magic brush that brings to life whatever he pictures.
[1. Painting—Fiction. 2. Magic—Fiction.]
1. Title. PZ7D3925Li [E] 80-11351

ISBN-13: 978- 0-8050-0801-2 / ISBN-10: 0-8050-0801-2
First published in hardcover in 1980 by Holt, Rinehart and Winston
First paperback edition—1993
Printed in Mexico

25   24   23   22

Long ago in China, a boy named Liang earned money gathering firewood and cutting reeds. His one wish was to paint. But he could not afford to buy a brush.

One day he passed an art
school and went in. "I want so
much to paint," he said.
"Please, will you teach me?"

"What!" The teacher glared at him. "A beggar wants to paint?" He drove Liang away.

But Liang could not keep his fingers still. When he went to gather firewood he drew birds in the sand with a twig.

When he went to the river to cut reeds he drew fish on the rocks with drops of water.

One night as he slept an old
man appeared on a phoenix and
placed a brush in Liang's hand.

"It is a magic paintbrush. Use it carefully," the old man said and flew away.

Liang jumped for joy. "Thank you so much!" he called after the old man. Immediately Liang began to paint.

He painted deer. As he finished, he saw that the deer came to life It really was a magic paintbrush!

"I will paint things for my poor friends," he thought. And he painted toy birds, horses, lanterns, and balls for the children.

And for their parents, things to cook with, furniture for the house, and tools for the field.

Then he went to the market-place and set up a table among the other merchants. And he made pictures of birds to sell. To make sure the birds did not come to life, he left something out.

One day a man asked for a picture of a crane. Liang gave it only one eye. But by accident, one drop of ink fell where the second eye should have been — and the crane flew away.

Now everyone knew about Liang's magic brush. Including the greedy emperor.

He went out with all his soldiers
to take the brush away from
Liang.

But Liang refused to give it up.

The emperor ordered him bound and brought to the palace.

There the emperor ordered Liang to paint a dragon. But Liang painted a toad instead. The emperor then ordered him to paint a phoenix. He painted a rooster instead.

Furious, the emperor seized the brush and ordered Liang imprisoned. The greedy emperor then sat down to paint mountains of gold. But they turned into rocks and rolled off the table.

The emperor tried again. He painted a large tree. But what do you think happened? It turned into an enormous python which nearly bit the emperor's head off.

Liang knew the brush would lose its magic in the emperor's hands. He thought of a plan. And he sent word to the emperor saying that in exchange for his freedom he would paint whatever the emperor wished. The emperor accepted.

"Paint me the sea," the emperor
ordered. Liang drew a sea.
"Where are the fish?" the
emperor asked.

Liang drew and drew and soon a sea full of fish were swimming about.

"So long as we have a sea," said the emperor, "let us have a boat!" Liang painted a boat, which was soon bobbing about on the water.

Delighted, the emperor called the royal family to come and join him on the boat.

"Get us some wind, so we can move," cried the emperor. Happily, Liang painted wind and the boat began to rock. "More wind!" the emperor cried. Liang drew more wind, and more. Soon waves were splashing and crashing over the deck.

"Enough!" the emperor cried. But Liang would not listen. He drew so much wind, the boat keeled over and broke into a million pieces. The emperor and the royal family sank to the bottom of the sea.

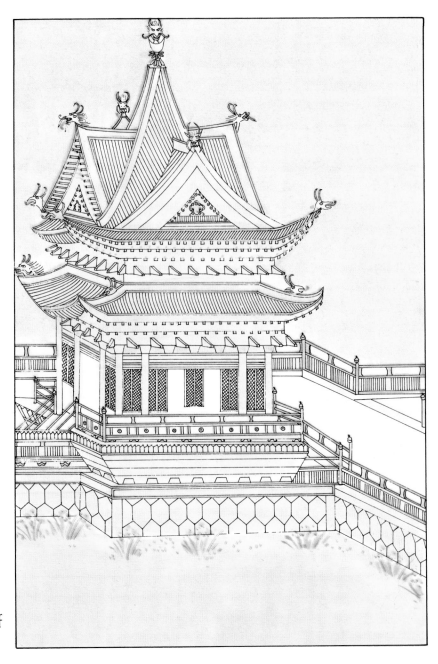

The story of Liang and his magic paintbrush spread far and wide. But what became of Liang? Nobody knows.

Some say that he went back to his own village. Others say that he roamed the earth painting for the poor wherever he went.

About the Author

A student of Corita Kent in California, Demi has traveled and studied art throughout the world. She has received several art awards, including a Fulbright Scholarship to study in India, and her diverse range of work has been exhibited from coast to coast and even abroad. Among the mediums she works in are serigraph, watercolor, mobile, collage, and textile design. The author and/or illustrator of numerous well-received children's books, including *The Empty Pot*, makes her home in New York City.